Lana J. Kimball
2582 Sun-Mor Avenue
Mountain View, Ca 04040

WORKING COTTON

WORKING

Harcourt Brace Jovanovich, Publishers

SAN DIEGO   NEW YORK   LONDON

COTTON

WRITTEN BY Sherley Anne Williams

ILLUSTRATED BY Carole Byard

Requests for permission to make copies of any
part of the work should be mailed to: Permissions Department,
Harcourt Brace Jovanovich, Publishers, 8th Floor,
Orlando, Florida 32887.

The text of *Working Cotton* is based on the poems
"the trimming of the feathers" and "conejo," orginally
published in *The Peacock Poems* by Sherley Anne Williams,
© 1975 by Sherley Anne Williams, Wesleyan University Press,
by permission of University Press of New England.

Library of Congress Cataloging-in-Publication Data
Williams, Sherley Anne, 1944–
Working cotton/by Sherley Anne Williams; illustrated by
Carole Byard.
p.   cm.
Summary: A young black girl relates the daily events of her
family's migrant life in the cotton fields of central California.
ISBN 0-15-200004-6
[1. Migrant labor—Fiction. 2. Cotton picking—Fiction.
3. Family life—Fiction. 4. Afro-Americans—Fiction.]   I. Byard,
Carole M., ill. II. Title.
PZ7.W668174Wo   1992
[E]—dc20   91-21586
Special Edition for Scholastic Book Fairs, Inc.
A B C D E

Printed in Singapore

Author's Note

Our shame as a nation is not that so many children work
the fields but that so few of them have other options,
that the life chances of too many are defined by the cycle
of the seasons. In environments characterized by
minimums—minimum wages, minimum shelters,
minimum food and education—individual character,
the love of a family, can only do so much; the rest is up
to the country.

—Sherley Anne Williams

The illustrations in this book
were done in acrylic paints on Stonehenge white paper.
The display type was set in Caruso Scratch Dot.
The text type was set in Berkeley Old Style Medium
by Thompson Type, San Diego, California.
Color separations were made by Bright Arts, Ltd., Singapore.
Printed and bound by the Tien Wah Press, Singapore
Production supervision by Warren Wallerstein and David Hough
Designed by Trina Stahl

For those who labor
on the land and the
children working beside
them
For John and
Jayvon, my own first
fruits
For the children of
the Valley
    — S. A. W.

For my brother, Michael,
the laborer who loves the
land — an inspiration.
    — C. B.

We gets to the fields early, before it's even light. Sometime I still be sleep.

It be cold, cold, cold.
The field fire send up a gray trail to the hazy sky. Everyone speak
in smoky whispers. "Don't get too close to that fire, Shelan."

This side warm, other side cold; both sides can't get warm at once. "Sun be out soon," Daddy say. "Burn off this fog and the dew."

Daddy pick the row side of Ruise and Jesmarie; they picking the row side of us.

Mamma keep the baby, Leanne, and the water jug on the row we be working. Mamma sing; Daddy hum.

I'm a big girl now. Not big enough to have my own sack, just only to help pile cotton in the middle of the row for Mamma to put in hers.

Cotton smell like morning, sometime, kind of damp. It smell
dusty now it's warm, like if you get too close, you sneeze.

The rows of cotton stretch far as I can see.

Daddy pick so smooth and fast. You see him reach for a bunch of cotton, then you see him pull his hand out the sack. The cotton's gone, *may be* in his sack, but you never seen my daddy put it there.

Daddy's cotton sack so long, they have to fold it double to weigh it. Take a long time to empty his sack into the trailer.

Mamma bring cornbread for lunch, and greens. Sometime,
it's a little piece of meat in your bowl.

It's always kids in the field; sometime they be your friend.
But you hardly ever see the same kids twice, 'specially after we
moves to a new field.

Jesmarie always be thirsty after we eats; then Ruise have to
have water, too. Mamma say, "You-all should drink at lunch."
Daddy say, "You girls stop playing around so much."

I wish I could still stay down at the end of Mamma's row and just only fetch the water jug and see at Leanne.

If I was old as Ruise or Jesmarie, I could pick fifty, even a hundred pounds of cotton a day.

It's a long time to night.

Daddy say cotton blossoms like any growing thing, only sometime cotton don't know when it be spring. Cotton flower this late in the year bound to bring us luck.

The bus come when it's almost dark. Us all be tired.
Daddy take the baby; Mamma take the bundle. Me and Ruise,
Jesmarie carry the sacks.

Lana J. Kimball
2582 Sun-Mor Avenue
Mountain View, Ca 94040